Out of Arkansas
1945

"A true story based on an outright Lie"

Villie 1945

Order this book online at www.trafford.com
or email orders@trafford.com

Most Trafford titles are also available at major online book retailers.

Note for Librarians: A cataloguing record for this book is available from Library
and Archives Canada at www.collectionscanada.ca/amicus/index-e.html

Printed in Victoria, BC, Canada.

ISBN: 978-1-4269-1937-4 (sc)

*Our mission is to efficiently provide the world's finest, most
comprehensive book publishing service, enabling every author to
experience success. To find out how to publish your book, your way, and
have it available worldwide, visit us online at www.trafford.com*

Trafford rev. 11/23/2009

 www.trafford.com

North America & international
toll-free: 1 888 232 4444 (USA & Canada)
phone: 250 383 6864 ♦ fax: 812 355 4082

Villie 1945

Chapter 1

THE OLD MAN HITCHED UP the horses to the wagon just the same as he had done for the past thirty years, only this time there must have been some thing different. I could tell by the way he was moving , his limp , his eyes were red as though he had been crying, what had brought this tough old man to tears, he had always been tough as nails?

I pulled at his coat, and he turned and said " jump son, where're guna be late if we don't cross the river fore noon, been rain'n up in the hills for two days now" I knew not to dilly any with this old man ,cause he had busted my butt many times just for asking a question.

I jumped into the old wagon as best as I could for a six year old but I still didn't understand the urgency to be traveling at five in the morning and still the old man hadn't finished unloading the corn stalks and a few scroungy looking corn ears from the back of the wagon bed. I didn't know at the time we were at war with a country called Germany, I thought Germs

were something we had to wash off before we got to the table. Anyway here we were bouncing along the trail at the break of dawn with the smell of fresh lilac in the air and the gray squirrels running across the road ahead of us, how could anything be wrong? He had promised to buy me a Heresy chocolate if I 'd quit tak'n so much.

As we rounded the bend I saw why he was worried about water and rain. The whole river bottom, The Washita was flooded for as long and wide as you could see. What was this old codger going to do? Drown us out of madness, or just plain ignorance.

Well what I didn't know was his son, my Uncle Dan was coming home. But I also didn't know why we had to pick him up in the wagon.

By the time we reached the river the sun was just starting to peck over the hill near Aunt Zoe's home stead. Now I didn't like floating this wagon and team across the river but the old guy was hell bent to get to Huddleston's Store for some reason and I knew I had a candy bar coming so I kept quite. As we were about half way across , the wagon started to float, then it turned side-ways in the direction and flow of the water, Here I was scared as hell, can't swim, too afraid to even scream, then the old man put his arm around me and said " It's ok, son, we guna make it". As he wiped his eyes again with his old red bandita.

Just as I thought this was the end of the world, the horses started to claw up the side of the bank and I almost fell out of the seat the way it bounced and rolled, then I felt that strong hand grab me again by the neck. Then he said" I don' t want to lose you too little feller".

I was starting to like this old guy a little better but why was so many people down at the saw mill that he owned so bitter at him?

What did he do? I had heard several times at night setting by the fire place when the elders were telling stories, that the old man had killed two young Green Chain workers for molesting one of his Daughters, the court had let him off on probation and to never again drink or make any more white litenin'. What, What was wrong? What was this stuff?

Remember, during this time period, most of the law was administered by the local sheriff and the local judge, unless one had money or other influence.

Grandpa knew a lot more about chemistry than most people thought and I did find out later that he had fought in WWI as some kind of a Demolition expert and had been to this place called Germany, but now he was just some kind of an old corn farmer, or was he?. What I didn't know at the time, he was one of the best corn whisky makers in the Ozarks during the prohibition period. He sold the stuff to some wholesale warehouse in Kansas City, labeled as Sorghum Molasses. He was doing a real profitable business until the laws were changed to make it legal again. When that folded, he went into the saw mill business just as the war was about to start.

Well that wasn't so bad but he loved women. He had one wife (Nettie) in the Kates'es Bend, the area we were in and another in Kansas City. The Grandma we knew (Nettie Maddelson) had three daughters, of which one was my mother and also a son, the one the old man and

I were going to pick up at the store across the river. Now there was another family in Kansas City I'll tell you about later, but now we were in a serious mood to get to this store at Pine Ridge and pick up Uncle Dan.

By the time the store was in sight the old man was starting to whip the horses and lather and foam was running down their backs and legs, now for some reason his whole mood had changed from sorrow to anger, was this some kind of a duel personality or what? As he raced up to the store I could almost see hell in his eyes. What was wrong?

He pulled the wagon up close to the loading dock at the front of the store next to a big long white pine box. What did we need this for?

Then it struck! Uncle Dan was in that box, we were going to take him home to the old family cemetery, where the rest of the Maddelson Clan was buried. I found later Dan was killed in the war or so the rumor was supposed to be, but in real facts as the court would finally show he was killed by his step father, my Grandpa John Vickers!, Well, not by his on hand, but he had it done. We'll cover that later!

What was actually in that pine box? Besides some burnt bones and a missing skull!

Chapter 2

GRANDPA JOHN HAD TO HIRE 2 men to help load the pine box into the wagon and this seamed strange because only the burnt remains of uncle Dan was supposed to be in that box. I did not know much at the time but after we crossed the Washita at a secluded spot, he opened the box, he wouldn't let me look but he did hold up some sacks of something that looked like sand or grain to me and I did find out later it was some type of blasting powder, for what? Did he have that many enemies or was this for some other job.

Each time I tried to enquire about the pine box, he would cut me off as this was all part of his personal business and I was too young to understand.

By the time we reached home that night it was getting

dark and the old man put the wagon and team into the barn and put a big lock on the door. He said tomorrow we will take the casket to the cemetery for the funeral.

At daybreak all hell broke loose, all 6 of his Coon Hunting dogs chimed in choirs to note the arrival of the local Sheriff and 2 Deputies were at our door to inquire about the heavy casket that was picked up at Pine Ridge yesterday.

The Old Man was at the door right away with his shot gun and mad as hell to be disturbed at this early hour.

"What do ya want sheriff ?"

Sheriff Cox tried to be nice but " I need to look at yer body you brought in last night cause something don't sound right as I hear tell"

"Sound right my ass, It's my own flash and blood"

"Maybe so, just need to look for my self"

"OK I'll show you"

They all took off to the hay barn and the Old Man opened it up and the Sheriff was surprised to see the barn locked out in this part of the country but inside they go and there sets the wagon with the new pine box on it.

"Open it up" said the Sheriff, I need to see what's inside.

The Old Man did as he was told and what did we see?,

A pile of burnt bones and 6 sacks of sand, nothing more.

The Sheriff turned to me and said " you were with your Grandpa when he picked up the body, what did you see ?"

Just being around some one of this authority was enough to make me wet my pants.

"Didn't see nothing, just a box to me"

The Sheriff knew some body was lie'n but what he didn't know was Grandpa

went back to the barn in the middle of the night to take out the blasting powder and replace it with sand bags. The bones were most likely that of some unknown soldier and Uncle Dan was not to be found till later, alive and" out to get" the Old Man and his other family in Kansas City.

The Sheriff was stumped and knew the Old Man well and would catch him in the act later, just need a little more time he thought to himself.

What was the purpose of killing Dan and also why the 6 bags of high explosives?

I didn't know the answers at that time but it all came to light in the near future.

The Sheriff and his Deputies went back to town and all was quite for several days as we buried Old Dan and the pine box as planed.

All the while this was going on, my Mother was in a state of terror due to the fact she was not a real citizen of the US at the time, an adopted daughter to the Old man. The Sheriff and the locals didn't know this.

My father John Clint, from the other side of the Washita river (Clint Family) had kidnapped her from the country of Mongolia while he was stationed there before the war and brought her home as a war bride and this is why I'm an American and not Mongolian also why she is of a darker color than her sisters. My father at this time was on his way back from California to pick up my

7

mother and I and return to the land of milk and honey as some of the Arkies had stated and only a few were able to migrate west, most were stopped at the Colorado river crossing due to the heavy influx of Okies and Arkies as they were called.

My mother Uel, replaced the real daughter of the Old Man on the county poles because his real Daughter(Nellie) was killed in his first liquor run to Kansas City around 1933. (More on this later)

He used his children to help promote his business and to camouflage his actions of ill deeds. In time it did catch up but not till he was well into old age.

The next week came the Sheriff again, arrested the Old Man and took him into Mena, the county seat to process the trial of killing and transporting explosives across state lines. Well it all looked good to the Sheriff and the local District Attorney but Old John had other plans.

He must have had more than 20 loyal friends working for him at the mill and other side line businesses that were willing to do what ever need be to

get him out of jail and keep their little flow of money coming in as times were hard for all the people in this part of the country.

The trial and prep work continued on for more than a month before a final hearing time was set. The next morning was the show down for the county to catch this Old Codger and nail him for good as he was responsible for several deaths in that area and some were not white folks either!

If you will recall Arkansas was one of the Confederate

states and they still felt that the Niggers were still sub-human. He wasn't prejudice, just a Supremacist.

To get a fair trial in any county within Arkansas, you had to go north or run the county! Run the county was one thing the Old Man had on a string or more said on the bottle (corn whiskey) He still made the stuff but only for trading favors.

The night before the trial, someone moved him out and into his place they put one of the old Nigger drunks.

Sure as hell some one blew-up the jail and killed the black man in his cell, John escaped in the night and went back to Kansas City till the thing cooled off a bit then returned claiming a loss of memory.

The whole town was getting upset about the lack of law and order and that Old John could get away with Murder.

Chapter 3

AROUND THE YEAR 1938, MY father, John Clint was working for Old John Vickers, my Grandpa, at his saw mill in Polk County as the mill electrician and general mechanic and good at it!

He was required to keep the mill running and a big demand was growing for rough shipping container lumber due to the possible German build up in Europe and the needed help the US was giving England just before WWII.

He had worked for the mill for over 3 years now but

did not like the things he saw and wanted out. An offer came from his father Ciefus Clint based on a reference from his former boss Mr. Henry Ford at Dearborn, Michigan.

Ciefus had worked for Old Henry in 1931 at the start of the new Model "A" and they became good friends based on a mutual joke Old Henry always Quoted:

"If it's got wheels on it or Tits on it you're gona have trouble with it"

This held true for almost everything we did in Washita Basin. All things seamed to revolve around " Horses, Wheels and Tits"

In 1937-38 Ford Motor Company was helping the Russians with farm tractors and assembly plants in the Volgograd and Caspian sea areas and Mr. Ford wanted to keep his operations intact. The US was also helping provide surveillance in the near by border town of Moran, Mongolia.

A British Radio Co. was building antenna tracking towers there and needed expert survival help with the power supplies and motors.

My father John Clint was sent there by the referral of Mr. Ford to help and for this young man to be called and sent to a foreign country was something very special! At a time when all others were just getting by, he was able to make an unusual showing and put himself into a little politics.

This is the point in history where I came into being:

My father had been working in Moran for about 6 months and there he met a pretty, young half breed daughter of the Project Manager. The manager was

British and his wife was Mongolian, they had 3 children of which Uel, my mother was the eldest.

As things do happen to young couples in love, she became pregnant and this was not a good thing!

In the Mongolian family rules, this should not happen till a marriage partner had been chosen by the girl's father.

Now my father was in deep stuff for a young man in a foreign country, no friends, not much money and pulling a dumb act of letting his brains fall between his legs!

Well this happens quite often as nature plays it games but in this country of nomads, it could cost you and the girl a death penalty if the chief so felt it proper.

My father's choice was to escape with the girl by horse back to the Caspian Sea and catch a freighter to England to the girl's relatives then by ship to Huston, Texas then by rail to Kansas City and hide out at Old John Vickers family and wait for the old man to come back.

When the news hit the fan the night John Vickers got back from one of his liquor runs in Mena, Arkansas, the old man was ready to have a real fit as none had seen before.

This young girl that my father had brought home was almost identical to the daughter he had lost in one of his first liquor runs back in "33" where Nellie was killed by cross fire of the "ATF" agents.

Old John didn't event know his daughter was dead till they were out of town. He thought she was just hiding and too scared, afraid to move.

He had been running the team and wagon at break neck speed to get away from all this confusion, the result

13

of all this was a loss of his liquor and the loss of his prize Daughter, Nellie.

This grieved him deeply and instilled a lasting hatred for the "ATF" until his dyeing days.

"Pay back is Hell" he always was quoting.

She was slim, trim and with black hair. He had a difficult time adjusting to the sight and memory of his losses. This new daughter was to take her place, was this in God's hands as his wife had just told him?

He was ready to kill off half the family at first and then his young new wife started to show the only control he understood. He had been away far too long and he needed some sympathy and love'n. She was able to get him to bed and liquored up enough to divert a clash that night. The next day Old John and my father John Clint were able to talk down the problem and go along with my father's plan of accepting Uel as his daughter and he in turn would go back to keeping his saw mill in Arkansas running, this in turn would keep the money and liquor flowing and allow Uel citizenship as his daughter.

The name Uel Nellie Vickers was put on the county tax rolls and John Clint

(My Father) had to make good his part of the bargain of make'n the mill run

and produce the needed lumber again.

War was brewing, Hitler had made his deadly move on Europe and the world would never be the same!

Chapter 4

I WAS BORN IN THE latter part of October, 1939 at my Grandmother's house in the Bend of the Washita on the old home stead and delivered by my grandmother Nettie Maddelson and totally looked after by her 2 daughters that were just a few years younger than my mother.

My mother was adopted by her and her second husband John Vickers of Kansas City, Missouri. They nicknamed me Smiley but my real name was listed to the county as Villie Clint as this was my father's last name and my mother used the name of her brother from Mongolia as my first name.

I did not get a birth certificate till I started to school in 1945 and it was kind of phonied up as there was no record of my birth till I needed one at the start of my first year in school. So, when asked at the hospital about my birth, they said " What do you need as for as information". My grandmother supplied all and that was the end of it, no other question asked, she paid the clerk $5 and I was legal, Ha!

Old Nettie was well known in the Bend as a Mid-Wife and Medicine Woman. Most people only went to a doctor if something was broken or beyond the cure of Cow suave or Witchcraft.

The good thing about being born in a place and area like this was, you could be anyone and born at anytime and still no one cared. Times weren't easy and people were not accounted for as well as they are in today's climate or electronic world. At this time only a pen and paper, a $5 dollar bill or a jug of corn whiskey solved most all legal transactions.

I started out as the only grand child in this family of three daughters and was pampered in every way. I guess I could do no wrong as these old ladies let me have the run of the house until my father or old grandpa came back, then the rules changed!

About 3 years after I was introduced the Washita area and America was in full bloom with WWII, my father was getting tired of the saw mill business. He and his younger brother, Aroby received a letter from their cousin Doc Clint in California telling about the land of milk and honey. They couldn't hold back any longer.

Hitching a rid by rail to California was an 8 day ordeal and consuming a lot of canned pork and beans along the way.

After 8 days of hell, they arrived by pure luck at Tipton, California in the San Joaquin Valley at Doc's farm, ready for the spring planting season of cotton and hard work. Irrigation and lots of machinery to repair.

Old Doc was a retired Veterinarian, and had invested in cotton farming in the early twenties while land was cheap. He was doing good except the war had taken all his young help away. He was glad to see them!

Doc made them a sleeping quarters above the pump house that was used for a junk storage room, cleaned it out and set-up two cots made from old cotton sacks. Now they could clean-up after 8 days and sleep under royal conditions, a clean bed and no bugs to sleep with. Only an old cat and a few hearty mice!

Lots of work and better money than Arkansas, long hours and no women!

Both brothers were getting lonesome for their wives!

Dad had saved most of his money and with in 6 months he sent for mom and I, with good seats on the Pullman coach to California. After 4 days and nights we set foot at as rail stop in Tipton, California, tired, no bathing and only the food we had carried with us.

Telephone service was almost non-existent this far out, so we hitched a ride with another old farmer to Doc's farm about 15 miles out of this little dusty town, arriving just as the sun was setting.

My Father and Mother were so happy to see each other they were crying and I had never seen a grown man cry before. I hardly recognized my father due to my age at the time, so this was no big deal to me.

My Uncle Aroby had moved north to another farmer some time earlier to a small town called Modesto and was working there and was planning on his wife to arrive in the near future with their young daughter.

With the pump house empty, we had the whole place to our selves, 12 ft. by 12ft. with a kerosene cook stove to boil water on and a small sink that drained down the side of the building to a flowerbed below. No running water but an outhouse not far away we could use as needed as the need arose.

"These new California comforts were a pleasure" My mother always would always say, compared to the old homestead or event Mongolia. She was happy to be with my father and he with her!

Our Cousin Doc was a good old man and so was his wife Cavella, God-fearing people and went to the local Free Will Baptist Church every Sunday. Except for one thing, Doc loved his liquor and seam to develop "Stunblin Pneumonia" from time to time as a result of this. This was one of the main reasons his two sons moved out and went to work in the shipyards in San Francisco. " Couldn't put up with his temper when he was lit up" they said.

They prayed for him a lot at the church, but to no avail. My father said " God won't help you unless you help your self" This was getting time for us to move again, he was starting to feel this for some reason.

With in 2 weeks dad found another job working a little further north for a rich diary farmer in the town of Reedley. Better pay and more working time as dad said, " I'm wasting 6 or 7 hours a night sleeping".

He was young, ambitious, and eager to learn, so the more he worked, the better he felt about himself.

We moved into a nicer place, one with 2 rooms, a kitchen with hot and cold running water and an indoor toilet. We really had come up in the world!

He worked for the Hammer family for about a year then advanced to the need at a widow's big ranch near by to run her ranch for her as her 2 sons were off to Europe to fight in the war.

The widow's name was: Mary Monetti, an old woman in her early 40's but she still looked good even at that Relic age! Her youthful looks was due in part to her Italian heritage and the consuming of her daily dose of fine red wine.

Occasionally, if I happened to be near her home, she would offer me a half ham sandwich and a small glass of this fine wine but I had to keep my mouth shut and not let my parents know of this because they belonged to the local Baptist church of which had a dim view of liquor as that was an abomination of God's will and he would surly strike Litni'n on your ass for this evil deed. It seamed OK to mess with the congregation's wives but no liquor!

This must have been a conflict of interest but the Holy Word had to be spread around to these heathern farm labor camps.

Old Mary was a devout Catholic, so the local Priest must have approved of this slogan her late husband had mounted to their kitchen wall just a short time before he died in 1935.

It stated: May friendship, like wine, improve as time

goes by and that we always have Old Wine, Old Friends and Young Hearted Women.

In later years of my life I found this slogan to be very true.

My father liked the farm work and the added responsibility he had acquired and wanted to settle down there but something always popped up to change his way of living.

About a year passed and my mother was pregnant with my new brother. They named him Dale and I could see this new addition was getting all the attention! He was born right after the war in the fall, after that excitement next my mother wanted to learn driving the family car, a 1936 Ford. She felt a need to be more mobile as some of the cousins were driving and she thought she needed to drive me to Kindergarten school also.

It was 7 months or so before she mastered her California license and more confidence to be an American.

Just as things started to smooth out, another crisis had developed at the homestead with Old John Vickers.

He was starting to drink up his profits from his bootleg liquor business and Sheriff Cox was on his case again. They caught him with a load going to Kansas City again, took his cargo and tried to lock him up but under some technicality, the Sheriff had to let him go again.

Uncle Dan was coming home from the war and Grandma Nettie wanted my mother to come back and help her as her 2 daughters had boyfriends now and she was stuck with trying to run the farm, control her daughters and keep Old John out of jail. Each time he'd get free, it was back to Kansas City again.

Grandma Nettie sent a telegram to my mother for "Help". Come back as soon as you can! "How could she refuse" as her Identity was at stake and an honor needed to be repaid for Old Nettie granted her Birth Certificate.

My father was pressured into driving her back to the Washita Bend. "I can't stay around that old codger much longer" he said but" I will take you back".

Chapter 5

DRIVING HARD FOR 5 DAYS and camping out at night.

Route 66 was a two lane nightmare. This trip was not easy, mainly I was required to behave myself and take care of my new brother, he was born last November and now this was early February of 1945.

He was a good kid at that time I'm sure but my inclination was to " send him back to the company he came from". I had my dog Thumper and we were much closer than any old kid brother!

The war was over but driving in remote areas and finding a place to camp at night was not fun and some nights we just got off the road as far as we could and maybe out of sight, then bed down on the back side of the car. Mom didn't get much sleep because she was always scared of the dark, coyotes, snakes and any thing that moved.

On the 5th. Night, we rolled into Mena, Arkansas at midnight, it's raining, cold and we still have 20 miles out of town to the Washita Bend Homestead. As we leave the out skirts of town, the road turns to mud and hell.

We made it across the first creek then another 6 miles to Kate's creek at the bottom of the hill that led to the homestead. The creek was up and very muddy. Just across half way, the engine flooded and there we sat in about a foot of nasty, cold water and it's dark as possum's ass.

Dad said, " we got to walk the rest of the way, get out." " Leave the car till tomorrow."

Here we go across the muddy water and up the last mile to Grandma's cabin and it's raining all the time. Where're all wet and having to walk for over an hour by the time we arrive a fine greeting of 6 old coon dogs at full howl and little Dale crying at the top of his lungs. Not to mention that Me an Thumper are about frozen.

Grandma Nettie was home alone but she quickly lit up a couple of coal oil lamps and racked the coals in the fireplace. Old John was in Kansas City and the two sisters, Millie and Jennie were staying in Mena with Aunt Mandi so they could go to church with her and meet with some of the "Pretty Boys" and maybe party up. They were old enough, nubile and ready to start the search for a mate.

Grandma's old cabin had 2 sleeping rooms and a big kitchen with a fireplace for heat, a small wood burning cook stove with an oven, no running water. Water had to brought in from the outside open well by lowering a bucket on a rope then haul it inside and set it on the counter, to be hand dipped. There was a sink that drained out through the wall that supplied water for the coon dogs and other animals that were brave enough to venture into this mad compound of crazy people and mad dogs.

The next morning, Dad walked over to the neighbors farm and got Nettie's

cousin to go and pull our car out and back home with a team of mules. Dad dried the electrical system out and started the car.

Now we had Wheels, Horses and dry Tits, according to Mr. Ford, now we're gona have trouble next!

We had peace and quite for three days, until Old John returned.

Nettie never knew when he would return from his travels to and from Kansas City.

The only electrical communication was across the river at Pine Ridge because at the homestead we had no electric or telephone.

Pine Ridge was 8 or 9 miles as the crow flies and about 10 miles by road or wagon trail.

Grandma couldn't drive a team and wagon and had to rely on her cousins to get around to Pine Ridge or to the city of Mena for supplies and medicine.

She was confined or handicapped to some extent but she enjoyed the peaceful atmosphere of her neighbors and cousins that lived nearby.

Only when a baby was ready to be delivered, or someone was sick beyond the healing powers of "white Litni'n" or "Cow Suave" did she venture away from her homestead. The homestead was left to her by her first husband John Maddelson after his death in 1934.

She had married into the Maddelson clan in 1915 as

a young girl from her family of Goodners in the nearby town of Norman, Arkansas.

John Maddelson was the father of her two daughters, Millie and Jennie and a son, Dan.

The children's father was half Indian as his mother was full blood Ouachita from the local tribe along the Wachita River.

The Old Grandfather, Maddie Maddelson homesteaded the section from the Federal government in the 1870's as his parents had migrated there from Tennessee as new land was being opened up for settling.

He sold horses to the US Calvary and timber for the railroad, then in later years sold cotton during WWI. He made a good living and was well respected in that part of the country. Several Blacks and Indians worked for his operation before the war. He treated them well and all the families in the Bend lived Quite well for that time period.

In the early stages of home steading he traded with the local Indians alone the Washita. Trading in horses, corn and grain and also whiskey.

In the process, the Chief had a young daughter he fell in love with that could speak Arkansas English. He offered the Chief 5 of his best logging horses for her. She was good at house work and fixing meat for drying and canning, he knew she would make a good wife. They were married the next year as was the custom due to the necessity of a Christian neighborhood, and also to be accepted in to the white community as a member, not a slave.

Her name was Ayler, she was strong and good looking

and bore him a son they named John, the man Nettie married for her first husband.

Then a daughter was born about 5 years later and lived till about 6 or 7 then died of some kind of fever. Less than a year later Ayler dyed of the same fever and Old Maddie was left in total turmoil.

Even though he was well to do at the time, he still needed companionship.

A short time later, he met his second wife, Dellar at a local funeral and they were married in a short time. She was a good woman for him and I remember her briefly in my visit to the Bend before the old man died.

She bore one son named Burr. I will return to his part of the story latter as he had an important part of claiming the homestead from my Grandmother Nettie.

Old John Vickers had found out about his stepson Dan arriving home from the war but he was as the story goes, killed in Texarkana, Texas in some kind of a bar brawl and while John was in Kansas City. word was sent to him to go pick up his box or body remains at Pine Ridge as it was shipped up to Mena then on to Pine Ridge.

It was his job to go and bring back the remains to his family and mother Nettie and collect something shipped along with the body.

Nettie was mad as hell for his staying away for so long in Kansas City, she refused to sleep with him for 3 days. He had to sleep on the old horsehair couch by the fireplace till my mother calmed them down.

Old John loved my mother Uel and would do almost anything she said. In fact, he loved almost all women, which was his problem.

Anyway, John got word that the box was on the dock at Pine Ridge and needed me or someone to go along with him to pick it up as our story started in the 1st. Chapter.

On the night of the jail break, two of Old John's workers from the saw mill stopped at the home stead and told Nettie they needed some special tools John had stored at the barn. They were there for quite some time and then returned out the main gate and said goodbye to Nettie and nothing was thought suspicious of it till the next morning when Sheriff Cox was at the door looking for John again. He was out of jail and gone!

Half of the jail was blown away and one man killed.

" What could have caused all this?" Sheriff Cox was about to find out!

Chapter 6

AFTER THE BLAST AT THE jail, Old John was bruised up a bit and could hardly hear anything but he stumbled south of town to the old feed store that was owned by his first wife's brother.

A horse was waiting, loaded with some dried food and some water. He was out of town in a short time, headed north to Fort Smith. If he kept up the pace, he could be in Fort Smith by noon tomorrow and catch a ride with one of the trucking companies that make their daily runs up Highway 71 to Kansas City. They owed him a favor he though to himself.

He had to stop and rest the horse several times and to give himself a break also for food and water. At the first stop he needed to verify the other bags of blasting powder, caps and black powder primer cord for lighting the caps was in tact, as he had ordered.

He didn't do blasting anymore but knew all the necessary details. Some people were willing to pay dearly for this information and the blasting powder that he had risked his life for in Texarkana, Texas 4 years ago. Now it was payday.

His Stepson Dan had helped with this maneuver by shipping a body remains home from the war, burnt from a shell blast and only the charred remains were sent home along with some of the sand, bones and whatever they were able to shovel up to ship. The box was addressed to some one in Pine Ridge that John had made up then used his Stepson Dan as the Military agent in charge for delivery.

Some where in this illegal move, Dan was wise enough to inquire and found out about John's past family and some of his illegal operations. Dan wanted a better cut of the catch and better treatment for his own family and Mama Nettie. John Vickers was not going to give in and made other arrangements ahead of time.

When Dan released the casket to the shipper in Texarkana, two men at the dock wanted to buy him supper and a drink before he left town. The men filed the papers for shipping to Mena and a release for Dan to sign. " We're all done here buddy, can we take you to the dinner and a party at the state line?" This was a curtsey of their Boss and he had been paid well. He was told to clean up any witnesses or people involved, this meant no witnesses.

The man listed on the death shipping papers was Daniel Meddel and the guy on site went by the name Dan Maddelson. This was close enough for them as they needed to finalize the request of their Boss.

"Com"on Dan the party's waitin, free food and drinks before you go on home"

"OK, just for a short one, I still have another days ride till I get home" After a little food and 3"short ones" Dan had to go to the restroom in the back of the bar and past the storage area. That's where the 2 dock hands jumped him.

Dan may have been young and with a certain amount of naiveté about himself but he was a lot tougher than the 2 dock hands that were getting ready to kill him. He was 6 foot 2 and 225 pounds with no fat. His father was half Ouachita Indian, he had a good background survival as a kid.

They both jumped him, pinned him to the floor, one pulled a long knife and was trying to use it on him. Dan had experienced this kind of fighting in his Army stint while in Germany, he was well trained in hand to hand combat. He knew survival skills well and was about to put them to action. He twisted the guy's wrist and turned the long knife back into his own ribs, as far as it would go and left it there. The guy let out a loud yell and slumped to the floor and quit breathing. All the while the other guy had him by the neck and chocking the living shit out of him. Dan makes a complete flip backwards, the guy's arm with him twisting it out of the socket, dislocating the arm from the shoulder creating total pain while demobilizing him completely.

Dan grabs his arm again and asks "Who put you up to this?" The guy could hardly breath but muttered "Vickers" " Please don't kill me!"

He dropped the guy and jumped through the back door with out even opening it, hitting the ground running. He knew now who he was looking for, " Got to get to Kansas City as quickly as possible" he said to himself.

Dan found his way to the bus depot and proceeded to get a ticket to Kansas City and to the root of this problem before Old John killed any more people or harmed his mother and sisters as they were still unaware of his other family in Kansas City. They knew only that he had a brother and some other relatives there from his child hood days. They didn't know he had two sons and a daughter that would have been the same age of Uel, my mother. He had exposed his daughter to gun fire and she died, then his wife died later in total grief as the result of his operations with illegal liquor. After his first wife died, he married a young girl that worked in one of the feed and molasses distributor warehouses where he sold his liquor.

This second wife, "Was a real charm" as he often quoted from time to time. She was the main reason to return to Kansas City on business. Of course money was the other reason, for one cannot operate two extremes with out a good supply of money.

Old John Vickers original family had nice living quarters above the warehouse his brother owned and operated. Feed and sorghum syrup distribution business was good and corn whiskey as a side line was also good for John.

They had two nice sleeping rooms, a kitchen and dinning with steam heaters. The steam was supplied by the grinding mill in the back of the warehouse. A full bath, a tub, cold and hot running water.

Why wasn't he content with this?

Why did he spend half his time in Arkansas in a poor area with an old sawmill? Money!!

"It takes money to make money" He always told Nettie.

This was part of his business before he met her and couldn't change it now, too many people depended on it. He was in too deep!

Chapter 7

MENA WAS A STOPPING POINT for him while shipping grain during the prohibition years.

He bought and sold many different foods and grains from the Texas side of Texarkana.

The Texas side was always more prosperous than the Arkansas side. More business, more investments and also more criminal actives.

In Texarkana, one could find or buy just about

anything. Money was the motivating factor of all forces, legal or illegal.

John had traveled this route many times and knew all the stops, hideouts and trusted places to stay.

John Vickers met Nettie Maddelson shortly after her husband John Maddelson died. He was looking for corn supplies and possibly some place to buy sorghum molasses to sell in Kansas City.

Nettie was in Mena looking at a local feed supply store for chicken feed and Veterinary supplies she used in her Midwife work in the back country of the Washita Bend.

Most people can be helped with the veterinary medicine at a lot cheaper rate. Animals are animals she said. She studied them and knew veterinary work and practiced on them as well as people.

Although she was not a Doctor or a licensed Midwife, she had a natural talent for healing and had built up a reputation as a good Midwife.

She was always friendly and never met a stranger it seamed.

Some times the sick only needed counseling and a friend to compliment the healing process she told my mother.

She and John were looking at the same brand of seed, and she said "Can't you see the writin Mister?"

John looked up with a smile, "Some times I kinda get my letters crossed Ma'm' was his reply.

"Maybe you'd be kind enough to help me?"

"I will if you can buy me a cup of that new coffee there're show'en off at the counter yonder"

"Got a husband do you Ma'm?"

"Did have till he passed away last year"

"Had a wife my self till last year" " She died of grief after my daughter was killed in an accident, just too much for her"

"Well Ma'm, My name's John Vickers" holding out his hand to her and trying to be polite.

"Mines' Nettie Maddelson, right pleased to meet ya"

Nettie could see the Old Codger was heart and weather beaten but still tough as a boot, all lean no fat and must have worked out side all his life.

His face, hands and arms showed long exposure to the elements.

He must be an Old Timer same as herself, forty-nine years of rough work and hell but still a lot of kikin left in her.

"Where's your home John?" replied Nettie.

Kansas City, Missouri at the moment" replied John.

"Why ya down in these parts?" she asked trying not to be too nosey but still to show some interest in the Old Guy.

"I buy and sell foods, grains, corn and molasses when I can find a good deal" "Been looking in this area for something new to take back home"

Nettie thought for a moment, "should I or should I not?" He seams to be a nice Old man, guess he'd be safe to visit with for a while.

Then she made the offer: "Well I have 40 acres of yellow corn planted and will be ready to sell in about two months if your back this way"

"Ma'm, shour would be happy to make you an offer when it's ready and sacked as this is the only way I can ship it." "I'll pay you a good price if it's clean and ready for grinding also"

"Good" Nettie said, "Give me your postal address and I'll give you the time to stop by and make an offer" "Bring your money though, cause I got other people that may want to buy it also and I got bills to pay as soon as I can sell"

"I'll do that miss Nettie"

They finished their coffee, shook hands and went about their other business.

She thought no more of it for a while, then the latter part of August he stopped by her home stead with out warning.

Old Chapter 8

JOHN HAD BEEN RIDE'N HORSES all his life and didn't like cars or trucks. You always have trouble withe'm. they drown out in the middle of creeks and rivers, you haft' a stay on the hard roads and they break down too much.

"We won WWI due to good horses" All the cars and trucks got stuck in the mud.

"Our Cavalry and foot solders always came through"

"A good horse is just the same as a good woman"

"Let the other folks use their fancy cars, I need a good horse"

He had rented this horse in town at a friend's stable, one of the few left around the country due to the advent of the automobile.

The roads were still a big problem in most areas, especially in the winter or spring thaw, only a horse could get you through to all parts he was having to go through.

For this particular day, a storm had blown in for the end of August. Most of the creeks and rivers were flooded but he was still able to get across at certain places providing access to the Washita Bend area to check on this new lady friend named Nettie. He had corn and a woman to look at!

She was a widow, had children and looked good for an Old Woman in her 40's. "Slim and ah bit sassy" He thought.

He didn't mind though, for he was used a bit himself.

Today, in particular, he needed some dry shelter, food, hot coffee and maybe a lady to visit with.

Ride'n up to the gate, he was greeted by several coon dogs as usual for most people in these parts, cause hunte'n was part of the process of putting food on the table, due to the depression and all. You don't just go to the store and buy something for supper at the flip of your hand. You either had to grow it, hunt it or steal it! Fairly simple in most cases and a bit risky in others.

In these parts, you could never come close to someone's house without arousing a dog alarm.

Nettie was at the door before he even got his horse tied to the gate.

Nettie's first reply was, "What ya doing out this far from the city John?"

"Are ya lost or lonesome?"

"Both" he yelled back to her above the claimer of the coon dogs.

"Come on in fore ya get your body a death of cold"

"Thank Ya, Nettie," "I'm glade I found your place and you at home"

"I don't like sleepe'n in some bodies hay barn"

"Well ya may hafta if you don't get cleaned up some"

"I'll get some water boiling for ya a bath if ya staye'n for She thought a while"of what she had just said and was ashamed to be so forward to this man she hardly knew. After all, she missed seeing a man around and hadn't event been close to one since her husband had died over a year ago.

Not that she really needed to bed one down or such, she just needed some companionship from time to time.

John stepped down from his horse, took her hand and kissed it.He didn't do this kind of thing very often and it even surprised himself.This must be something special. Why am I doing this?

She could tell he needed some attention,"He even smelled like his horse""Probably bathed just as often"At any rate, I can fix this Old Boy , if he'll let me, she was thinking.

"Come on in, John, this is Saturday nite, my kids are across the river at Pine Ridge"There're at the Sunday Social Church, be backtomorrow nite. "Nobody home but me and the coon dogs.

"I'll fix you some supper while the bath water is heate'n.

" Come prop your feet up"

"Put your horse in the barn for the nite"

"I'll find a spot for ya to sleep in after I've fed ya"

"Hope you come with an offer for my corn"

"I did, Nettie and been thinke'n bout you also"

"Ya have now, have ya?" "Why would that be?"

"Well you done something to my mind ah while back and I didn't forget it"

"That's mighty romantic, John, come on in, we'll have supper shortly"

She didn't have any fancy foods, just pinto beans with hog joule for meat, some garlic, fresh potatoes, onions and cold slaw cabbage. "Nothe'n fancy ya hear?"

Nettie was a tough business woman. She also knew how men thought when trading with a woman.

A woman can get a better bargain if the man is well fed.

Another thing she learned: A man is always soft hearted when hard and hard hearted when soft!

Chapter 9

AFTER THE JAIL BREAK, OLD John made his way out of Mena by horse back going north to Fort Smith in two days of hard riding. Still stopping at various points to rest and give his horse a break for food and water. He needed to stop for his own interest also as his age was starting to show, " I'm too old to keep doing this, he thought to him self"

At the out skirts of town, he left the horse with a farmer he had been trading with. The Old farmer gave him a ride into the industrial part of Fort Smith with his old Ford pick-up truck, dropping him off at the transport truckers dock that he had been using for shipping grain north to Joplin, Missouri and also to Kansas City, Missouri.

This company had trucks going north each day and he knew a ride was always available.

John went to the back storage area till 6 AM, got up and used the wash room to clean up and wash his face with cold water, now he was ready to catch a driver to Kansas City.

Grabbing his two back pack bags with the food and explosives, he was assigned to a rig going north on a big Mac tractor rig with a nice quite older driver. The old driver didn't know him, other than that he was some old farmer that needed a ride to Kansas City.

The truck continued north on Highway 71, stopping at different points to unload and take on various packages as needed along the way. Picking up supplies at Fayetteville, Arkansas, then on to Joplin, Missouri, pick up farm equipment tooling then on to Kansas City.   In the process of one and a half days of rough driving. Too much worry and not enough sleep for John!

He didn't know what to expect on arrival but nothing serious developed, good luck so for.

The driver dropped him off close to the feed warehouse his brother owned. He tipped the driver a $10 bill and thanked him for his friend ship. He was happy the driver did not ask a lot of questions.

Carrying his two packs to the back of the warehouse, around the corner, he faced the stairs leading to his apartment and home. With a sigh of relief, he was home!

By the time he was half way up the stairs, the door opened, at the top on the platform was his young wife, Sally. She let out a scream and with open arms and said: "You're back" "I heard you was dead"

"Not me Sally" "I still have 9 lives left, like a cat"

"I heard also that Nettie's son Dan, is looking for you"

"Dan?" "How can that be?' "We just buried his remains about 3 weeks ago!"

"Don't know, but he's alive and mad as hell"

"He's looking for you and wants some answers!"

"Can't believe this, I was told he was dead or had disappeared, his remains was sent to me at Pine Ridge a while back"

John asked about his sons, Ted and Jim. Last he heard they were still working across town at the lumber mill. Sally had not heard from them in over a year. Ted and Jim, both in their late thirties, were near the same age as Sally, his wife.

They were good boys, but stayed away from the Old Man's business. They knew the way he treated the people he traded with and that he had another family in Arkansas.

They had been on their own after John's dealing with the liquor and loosing his daughter Nellie and wife Mary in the "ATF" raid over 10 years ago. They still had a grudge and hatred for him over that. The two boys stayed away completely, no news or contacts for well over 7 years.

Now, John had a new problem, what to do with Dan here in town looking for him. Dan was supposed to be out of the picture!

Sally started making bath water and mixing up some

food. John hadn't slept much in the last 4 days and still couldn't hear very well either, his ears were still ringing from the jail blast. He also wanted a bath and sleep for a while.

He woke with a load on top of his body, Sally was sleeping on top of his chest, totally nude and breathing heavily and his nose was stuck right between her breasts.

"Now that he was rested, he could use some of that!"

She was well built for an old girl in her late 30's. She had never had any children and for the past 10 years, he had not used any protection while exploring her fine body. Something of nature had caused her to be dormant or unable to conceive, although he would have been happy to provide a child with her. They were happy to lay connected for several hours enjoying the warmth and wetness.   To day, he had other problems to deal with and at any moment that made him nervous of the fact that "Dan" might start rapping on the door.   Then he thought, "Where did I leave my bags?"

"Sally where are my bags?"

"In the back room where you left them last night"

"Oh God, thank you" "I have a lot of important things in there"

"Yes, I know, I checked them out last night while you were sleeping"

"Looks like you are getting ready to do some side line of work again"

"How would you know?"

"I'm not dumb!" "I know more about you than you give me credit for"

"I can do other things besides draw away all your energy with love"

"Oh thank you Sally, I do appreciate you and all the things you do"

"Some times I have too many things going on at one time and fail to recognize my blessings" " Sorry about that"

"I have done a lot of bad things I'm sorry for but I can't change that now" "I'm getting older and need another chance to make it right. Many of my deeds are catching up"

"Each time I leave you, I think this will be my last time to enjoy your beauty and what you do for me"

She rolled over and off of him, to the side of the bed, stood up letting the sun shine through her naked legs as she started to dress.

"I'll fix you some breakfast now before you leave"

"Do you want any thing extra, food or supplies for your saddle bags?"

"Yes, I'll take water and dried meat or fish if you have it" "Nothing else, I have to travel lite as possible till I have settled up with Dan, then I'll be back in a day or so.

"You will need to stay inside, out of sight and don't talk to anyone" "Do you hear?"

"Yes, I'll be" OK" though"

He finished his breakfast, grabbed his saddle bags and left without even giving her a hug, just a soft goodbye!

Chapter 10

DAN HAD BEEN IN TOWN for two days and knew the Old Man was hiding out or either out looking for him. He didn't know they were destined to meet at some time in the near future.

The issues had to come to a head. Dan was sure of this.

The Old Man was sure of this also and wanted to call a truce, make it right and make a settlement. What ever was needed, now old age was starting to show and he was getting tired of living two lives, two women and too many nights without sleep.

Dan had rented a cheap room with hot water and a bath at the outskirts of town near the old river park by the Missouri River crossing. He was hoping to resolve this issue without further blood shed.

This was a sleazy one room hotel used mostly by the service boys and the low end of society.

Several bars were close that catered to the boys coming home from the war and they served hot sandwiches. Transportation was near by the trolley system that ran all the way to the docks. He could wait this out for several days if need be till he was able to locate Old John.

John wasn't just hiding out, he was also looking for Dan in the process. He had a "crow to pick", they need to reconcile their differences and come to a just understanding equitable to each man and all concerned. "Other lives were at stake also"

Now, Dan had spent three nights in this ratty hotel by the river chasing the leads to locate Old John, still nothing and now he would go back to his apartment another time and wait in the woods behind the place.

His first day in town was to locate John's place and living quarters. He found the apartment and his "Lady" above the feed warehouse. Now he felt sorry for "Sally" and knew she was telling the truth and just an innocent bed partner involved in this fiasco.

She had not seen him, lately but she did hint that he was due back home any time. Two days had passed, now it was time to go back.

This time, he would try later at night with hopes of catching him. He would try later in the day near sun down. Hiring a cab due to the distance of 5 miles or more back to the feed warehouse. He had the cab driver wait and if he failed to return within a half hour, the driver was to call the police. He paid the driver $10 to wait and he would pay the balance later if no problems arose.

Stepping out of the cab, at the feed warehouse, he

looked up to the second floor windows that he knew was John's apartment, the lights were being turned off.

Someone was there! Walking to the back stair way quickly, he heard some noise but nothing unusual, He made it to the top and knocked several times before Sally opened the door with a frightened look on her face.

"Hello, what do you want?"

"I'm still looking for John"

"He was here two days ago right after you had stopped by"

" He stayed one night and said he was going to try and find you"

"Can I come in and look?"

"You can look if you want but you can't stay"

"I won't harm you Ma'm" Pushing his way into the entry and looking around in all directions, then heading to each of the bed rooms.

Glancing at a chair with some dirty clothing that belonged to a man, he was aware that some man was here but were is he now?

He was on the right track but where to find the Old Geezer now!

Dan started to leave, then said: "Ma'm, if he comes back or you hear from him, tell him we have to settle this peacefully" "I won't heart him, just need to settle the differences"

Sally stepping back in fear with her hand up against her mouth said, "Yes sir, I will tell him"

John's main reason to get back to Kansas City was the two bags of explosives he carried in his saddle bags.

Each bag was worth $5,000 to the new group of protesters that had just set up an office in town. They were upset at the way commerce was conducted on the Missouri River. The "ATF" were conducting searches of all cargo and possible gun and liquor trafficking by some of the local Indians.

John didn't have to do anything except make a drop at a predetermined point, they would do the rest.

His money he would find at the base of the stairway to his apartment behind the feed warehouse. Payment in $20 gold peace coins, a total of $10,000, no questions asked and no tracers, all in small bags of 50 coins each equaling $1000 each. A total of 10 bags.

He hated the"ATF" with a passion and was happy to deliver a "Payday"

Dan had to settled with in a proper family manor. No more blood shed! Now he had to do the right thing with Dan and his Mama, Nettie.

The next day, John returned home at the feed warehouse after he had dropped off the explosives at the spot near the city park under the rail base crossing the Missouri River.

By this time the sun was setting, allowing him time to enter his apartment without any workers around and arouse any other suspicion or any one to recognize him.

He grabbed the heavy tote bag at the base of the stairs, started to make several steps, then, from the back area near the woods came a voice from a man. "Hello John"

As he came closer, he could recognize the person as Dan. "Now what?" he thought to him self, he never carried a weapon due to his other clashes with the law. John was very strong for a man in his fifties. He had learned hand to hand combat in the 1st. World War. He really didn't need a gun for defense, he could kill a man with a snap of the neck and with no sign of blood or burses.

Although he had not killed anyone in several years, there was no doubt in his ability to use it if pressured into it.

He always claimed to be innocent and needed no defense allowing an easy excuse to defend himself in court.

"Hello my son!" "Are you OK?"

Dan's reply: "I don't want you to call me son any more!"

"I'm sorry Dan, I'm trying to make it right with you"

"It's more than ME!" " Mama needs help at home and we need better water and the "REA" electric will come to our area and our house with a little help"

"You can help with this or don't expect to have a place to stay when you come back"

"Don't expect the Sheriff to give you any sympathy either"

"I'll do everything possible to have you locked up, except kill you"

"I'll leave that up to your neighbors!"

" OK" "OK" " I am sorry, and now I want you to know I can offer you something for you part of the bargain"

He pulled a small heavy bag from his tote bag, "Here's 25 gold coins for you and 25 for your Mama." "That's $1000 dollars for your service"

"I'll be back in a week or 10 days to try and clear my name with the courts in Mena as soon as I can get in touch with Dick Huddleston's lawyer, Sam Kates, in Pine Ridge to take my case"

"If you can help me, I'll help you"

"OK, John, pay me and don't try to remove me from the picture any more"

"If you do try, I'll take you with me, Understand?"

"Yes I understand" " I'm truly sorry, we need to work together from now on, I need your help more now than ever"

"Things aren't getting any better with the way the government is worrying about the Communists taking over"

Chapter. 11

KANSAS CITY HAD BECOME A focal point for the "ATF"
They were picking on anyone to justify their existence.
The city sat on a major shipping point of the Missouri
River, connecting to the Mississippi with barge service to
the Gulf of Mexico.

Now, that the laws on liquor had been legalized, the
war over, the "ATF" needed another enemy to chase and
keep their Agents busy.

The new opposition party that started during the
Depression, was called the "Socialist of America". No
doubt, some actually were Communists. Even the well
known Lawyer, "Sam Kates" from Pine Ridge was aware
of their activity as he was a close friend to another
attorney" Melvin Beli" at Berkeley, California. the
two often communicated about the rising problem of
Communism. Melvin Beli was hired by the "FBI" while
he was a student at Berkeley to do infiltration work with
the students during the start of the Depression, 1933-34

to try and find info regarding the "Social Welfare State" that J. Edger Hoover had so often spoke about.

Hoover was a total skeptic about anything that was different than total "Republicism".

Hoover suspected the infiltration of the Communist Party from the Russian Immigrants that were so prevalent at this time period. The Depression was no help in this matter either.

People were getting tired of this type of government system. No help for the Farmers, the poor, the working class and no hope in sight for the future. Even with the 1st. term of Roosevelt, Congress was still dragging it's feet.

Some unions were backing the Socialists also. The Socialists were not against the use of subversive force to accomplish their goals or to get a point across.

This is where John Vickers came into play. His main allegiance was to himself but if it gave anything in the way of "Payback" to the "ATF", he was more than happy to oblige.

The Agent in charge of the Kansas City region was an old government enemy of John's from the slaughter of his daughter back in 1933. His name was "Tom Mossback" and went by the name of "Mossy".

One of John's requests while shipping the explosives to the Socialists was, "Try to take Old Mossy out with you at the time of his raids" The Socialists main demolition guy, "Vic Cabinov" was an old friend of John's from their work together during WWI, John and Vic had worked in a small German border town of Cham, just east of a big city called Regensburg. They were both young then, around their mid 20's. Their job was with the demolition crew assigned to disrupt the German tank route that led into Czechoslovakia, a small border town called, Domazlice. They became good friends and John also helped him with his immigration papers after the war when he landed in Kansas City in 1920. Vic Cabinov had worked his way up in the party and had not forgotten John. The party had plans to disrupt the commerce on the Missouri in retaliation to the raids of the "ATF" on the local shippers. It was Vic's job to locate and carry out these plans. John didn't want to be involved with any kind of terrorist activity until he found out who was causing the problems. The "ATF" he was told and "Old Mossy" was in charge of it. "Count me in" was John's reply, "What do ya need?"

The party had a good supply of money but needed some of the new Simplex Plastic Explosive, that only the military had access to. John knew how to make the Simplex from the safe powder that could be shipped through the authorities and locals without detection. This is what he shipped to the Socialist group and they paid very well. In Gold cash, not COLD CASH! Twenty Dollar Gold Coins! The two barges heading up river by tug pusher were loaded with a general mix of cargo, nothing illegal from New Orleans. The main thing Vic Cabinov knew in the cargo that would catch the eye of the "ATF" was the use of a lot of old ammunition boxes to ship foundry castings for a farm equipment machine shop in Kansas City. Vic was able to check the freight manifest from the Harbor Master's list two days earlier and put a bug in the "ATF's" ear. He was able to get aboard one of the barges at a service stop earlier up the river at the capitol, Jefferson City. As night time approached he boarded undetected, planted the explosives mix with an adjustable timer that tripped when the covers were removed. It could be reset if caught with-in 10 seconds, otherwise only you and God knew the final timing.

Vic didn't want to kill any innocent people but it was very important to get their point across and to help send "Mossy to Hell" and inflect as much fear as possible into the local police as to discourage any further help to the "ATF".

They were not liked at all by the locals, the police included. The two barges were pushed into the docking area at 6AM the next day after leaving Jefferson City. The dock crews tied everything off and the Tug crew signed in to port and went into town.

At 7AM the regular unloading crews started setting unloading ramps for the lift trucks to roll onto the barges.

Just before unloading was to began, two black "ATF" cars arrived as Vic had planed . Two men from each car jumped to the docks with machine guns, stopped all traffic.

Next, out jumps "Old Mossy" with a hand held Red Spot Light.

"Everybody Halt, this is an inspection by the "ATF"!!!!

From the rumors he had intercepted, he was sure he had found some illegal fire arms or machine gun parts from the Army Surplus sale in New Orleans a few weeks back.

Mossy was a "smart ass" old agent and didn't mind walking over anyone to accomplish his goals. It was said:

"He would arrest his own mother if it put a feather in his hat".

Old Mossy jumped from the docks onto the first barge and started pulling tarps that covered the cargo. He didn't find much, so he called the other 3 men from the patrol cars to help check off the cargo on barge #1. He hopped over to the next barge #2 and started pulling tarps again.

Then he heard a snap sound, then a fizzle sound, turning around, he then recognized the flashing of a black powder primer cord burning, then a bright white flash, then Jesus!

The blast took out half of the barge, totally vaporizing his body and blowing the other agents into the river.

Grain, tools and other cargo began to rain down on everyone and all over the docks.

Vic was standing two blocks away with binoculars watching with a grim smile on his face.

"Pay back is Hell", He said under his breath. "Savas" He lifted his hand as if to make a toast in Russian with Vodka, a cold toast to "Mossy" John had made his "Payday", "An eye for an Eye", Now God had blessed his lost daughter Nellie.

Vic now had to get away to a safer place and inform John of the "Payday".

With in an hour, every Policeman, Sheriff and "ATF" Goon would be at the docks looking for old Mossy, this would take two or three days. They had to find what or who caused this and the Socialist Party was most likely to blame along with the Russian sympathizers.

Will Clift

All that really mattered was, "God called Old Mossy home!"

The next day Vic stopped to visit John and Sally at the feed warehouse apartment to have a toast to the final farewell of their old enemy Mossy.

Now John had other plans to attend to in Mena and try to clear his name, recover his

stepson's confidence and get his saw mill back into full production.

His long distance horse rides were over.

The young women and fast horses were about to kill him. He needed some Old Whiskey and an Older Woman for a while.

Now he had enough cash to hire Sam Kates to work on his side of the story of self-defense.

The new electric association "REA" was starting to run power in to the Washita Bend. Now was his chance to "Make it Right" with Nettie and her son Dan.

They needed electricity and running water and an indoor bathroom. More privacy while he was home with her.

If he could sell the old saw mill, they would move "Out of Arkansas" Some place near Dan on the Red River at a town called Gainesville, Texas.

This move may give Nettie a better place to raise her daughters and retire.

John Clint had taken his step daughter Uel and his only grandson to back to California, left his mill to be run by a bunch of clowns and he was getting to old to do all these things alone.

He still had Sally to look after in Kansas City and his

trading was a little slow but he needed to get into a slower pace anyway.

About the Author

WILL CLIFT GREW UP IN this area and has made some interesting comparisons to the present day lifestyle.